To C & C - always follow your dreams!
-A.K.

Dedicated to all of the
sporty girls out there.

- P.E.

# The
# Sporty
# Little Spider

By Patricia Esperon

Illustrated By Amy Klein

**The Sporty Little Spider**

**Huskies Publishing**

Text©2020 Patricia Esperon
Cover and Interior Art©2020 Amy Klein

All rights reserved, including the right to
reproduce this book or portions thereof
in any form whatsoever.
For information, e-mail the publisher at:

Huskiespub@gmail.com

Library of Congress Control Number: 2020948202

Author's Edition

ISBN
Hardcover: 978-1-64372-075-3
Softcover: 978-1-64372-078-4

The Sporty Little Spider
strapped on her water skis.
She was splashed by a wave,
and fell to her knees.

She held onto the rope
attached to the motor boat,
Then the Sporty Little Spider kept
herself afloat.

The Sporty Little Spider sat down on the chair lift.

She rode down the slope,
right into a snowdrift.

The snow blew away, and when she could see, The Sporty Little Spider went boarding through the trees.

The Sporty Little Spider
looked up at the rock wall.

She tried to make it up,
and took a little fall.

She scouted all around, and found a better way, then The Sporty Little Spider climbed up all the way.

The Sporty Little Spider peddled up the biking trail. Out jumped a bear, and off her bike she sailed.

The bear ran away, and when the trail was clear, The Sporty Little Spider rode on without a fear.

The Sporty Little Spider
pushed off of the dock.
She began to paddle
down, and got stuck on
a rock.

She used all her strength, and got the kayak free, then The Sporty Little Spider paddled happy as could be.

The Sporty Little Spider
climbed up the mountainside.
She hurried to the edge,
ready to hang glide.

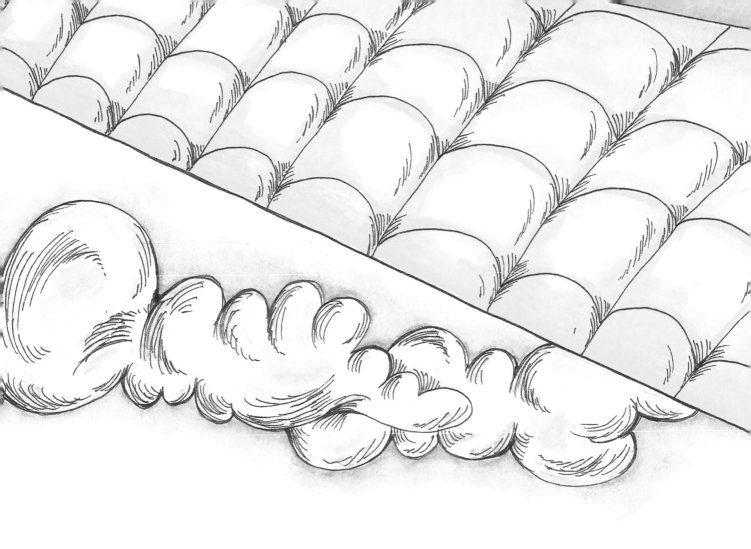

She took a deep breath, and next
she closed her eyes.
Then the Sporty Little Spider
floated up into the sky.